PRETEND YOU'RE A CAT

By JEAN MARZOLLO

Pictures by JERRY PINKNEY

Dial Books for Young Readers *New York*

Published by Dial Books for Young Readers,
A Division of Penguin Books USA Inc.
375 Hudson Street
New York, New York 10014

Text copyright © 1990 by Jean Marzollo
Pictures copyright © 1990 by Jerry Pinkney
Typographic design by Jane Byers Bierhorst
Printed in Hong Kong by South China Printing Company (1988) Limited
N
First Edition
1 3 5 7 9 10 8 6 4 2

Library of Congress Cataloging in Publication Data

Marzollo, Jean.
Pretend you're a cat | by Jean Marzollo
pictures by Jerry Pinkney. p. cm.
Summary | Rhyming verses ask the reader
to purr like a cat, scratch like a dog,
leap like a squirrel, and bark like a seal.
ISBN 0-8037-0773-8.—ISBN 0-8037-0774-6 (lib. bdg.)
[1. Animals—Fiction. 2. Stories in rhyme.]
I. Pinkney, Jerry, ill. II. Title.
PZ8.3.M4194Pr 1990   89-34546   [E]—dc20   CIP   AC

*The full-color artwork was prepared using
pencil, colored pencils, and watercolor.
It was then color-separated and reproduced as
red, blue, yellow, and black halftones.*

For Kirby Thornton Little
J.M.

To the children of Childrenspace,
thanks for your help and enthusiasm
J.P.

Can you climb?
Can you leap?
Can you stretch?
Can you sleep?

Can you hiss?
Can you scat?
Can you purr
Like a cat?

What else can you do like a cat?

Can you bark?
Can you beg?
Can you scratch
With your leg?

Can you fetch?
Can you roll?
Can you dig
In a hole?

What else can you do like a dog?

Can you jump?
Can you leap?
Can you swim
As you sleep?

Can you nibble
And look
At a worm
On a hook?

What else can you do like a fish?

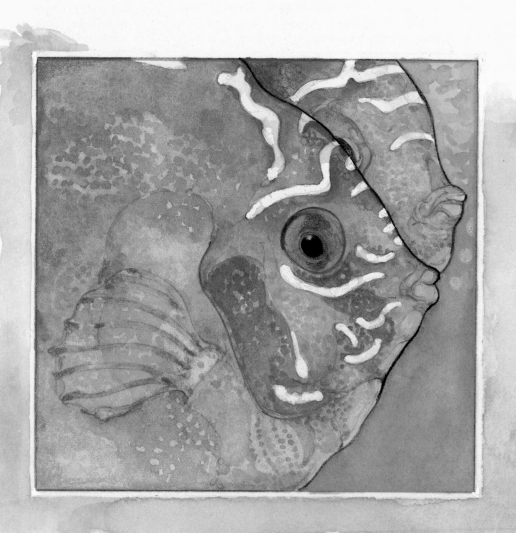

Can you fly?
Can you buzz?
Are you covered
With fuzz?

Can you land
On my knee?
Can you sting
Like a bee?

What else can you do like a bee?

Can you peck?
Can you pick
At a shell
Like a chick?

Can you scratch?
Can you cheep?
Can you hop?
Can you peep?

What else can you do like a chick?

Can you perch?
Can you fly?
Can you soar
In the sky?

Can you chirp?
Can you tweet?
Can you sing
With a beat?

What else can you do like a bird?

Can you chatter
And flee?
Disappear
In a tree?

Can you run?
Can you twirl?
Can you leap
Like a squirrel?

What else can you do like a squirrel?

Are you pink
As a bud?
Can you lie
In the mud?

Can you root?
Can you dig?
Can you snort
Like a pig?

What else can you do like a pig?

Can you chew?
Can you munch?
Can you moo
During lunch?

Can you drink
from a pail?
Touch your ear
With your tail?

What else can you do like a cow?

Can you snort?
Can you neigh?
Can you eat
Grain and hay?

Can you open
The gate?
Can you run
With your mate?

What else can you do like a horse?

Can you balance
A ball
On your nose
And not fall?

Can you dive
For your meal?
Can you bark
Like a seal?

What else can you do like a seal?

Can you wiggle
And glide?
Can you slither
And slide?

Can you head
For the lake?
Can you swim
Like a snake?

What else can you do like a snake?

Are you big?
Are you brave?
Can you sleep
In a cave?

Can you sniff
At the air?
Can you roar
Like a bear?

What else can you do like a bear?